The Biggest Little House in the Forest

by Djemma Bider
Illustrated by John Sandford

Art Direction by Carlo DeLucia

Caedmon

New York

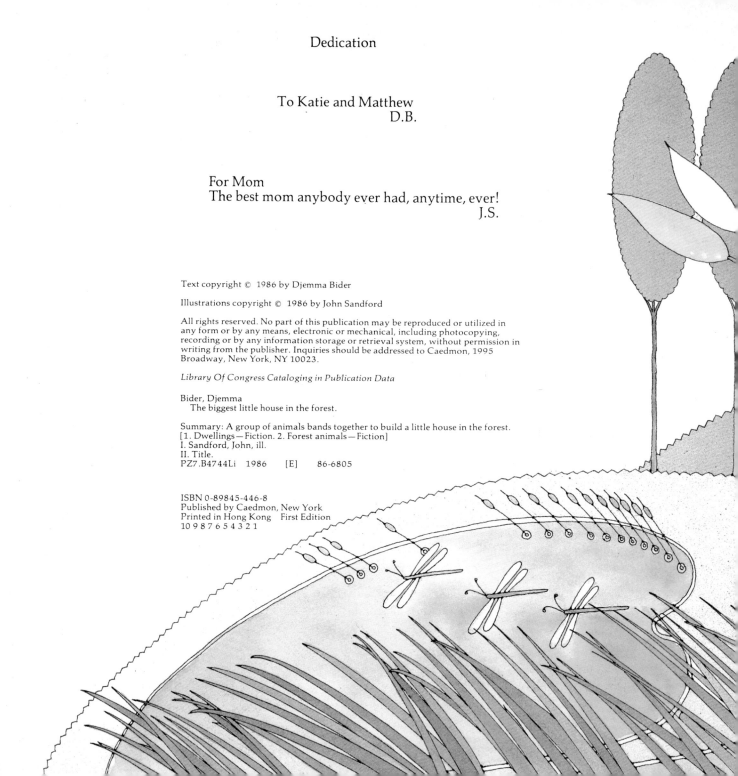

Dedication

To Katie and Matthew
D.B.

For Mom
The best mom anybody ever had, anytime, ever!
J.S.

Library Of Congress Cataloging in Publication Data

Bider, Djemma
  The biggest little house in the forest.

Summary: A group of animals bands together to build a little house in the forest.
[1. Dwellings—Fiction. 2. Forest animals—Fiction]
I. Sandford, John, ill.
II. Title.
PZ7.B4744Li 1986   [E]   86-6805

ISBN 0-89845-446-8
Published by Caedmon, New York
Printed in Hong Kong   First Edition
10 9 8 7 6 5 4 3 2 1

It was spring. The trees in the forest were turning green. A pretty butterfly was playing and having fun, flying and swooping. She looked down and saw a lovely little house in the thick grass.

When she peeked in, and saw no one lived there, she thought:

"What a nice little house! I will live here!" And so she did.

One day a mouse ran by and noticed the pretty little house.

"What a nice little house this is," she said. "But who lives here?"

"I live here," said Bernice the butterfly. "And who are you?"

"I am a mouse, and everyone calls me Millie. Will you let me stay in your little house?"

5

The butterfly thought for a while and then said:
"Come in, Millie. You're welcome to stay!"
And the two of them set up house together.

One day it was raining. A frog splashed
through the mud. He came hopping to the entrance
of the little house and rang the bell.

"Ribbit, ribbit, who lives here in this little house?"

"I, Bernice the butterfly, live in this house."

"And I, Millie the mouse, live in this house. And who are you?"

"I am a frog and my name is Fred. Will you let me stay with you?"

8

The butterfly and the mouse looked at one another and said:

"Welcome! Two of us is good. But three together is even better."

And so the three of them started to live together.

One day, a rooster was walking in the forest when he came upon the little house. He stopped, flapped his wings, stretched his neck, and suddenly called:

"Cock-a-doodle-doo! Who lives in this little house?"

Now, everyone who was inside came out and introduced themselves.

"I am Bernice the butterfly."

"I am Millie the mouse."

"And I am Fred the frog."

Then all together they asked him:

"And who are you?"

The rooster, feeling very important, shook his comb and cried:

"Cock-a-doodle-doo! I am a rooster and my name is Rudy. I would like to live with you."

And all together they said:
"And we would like to have you live with us, too!"
So all four of them started to live together.

15

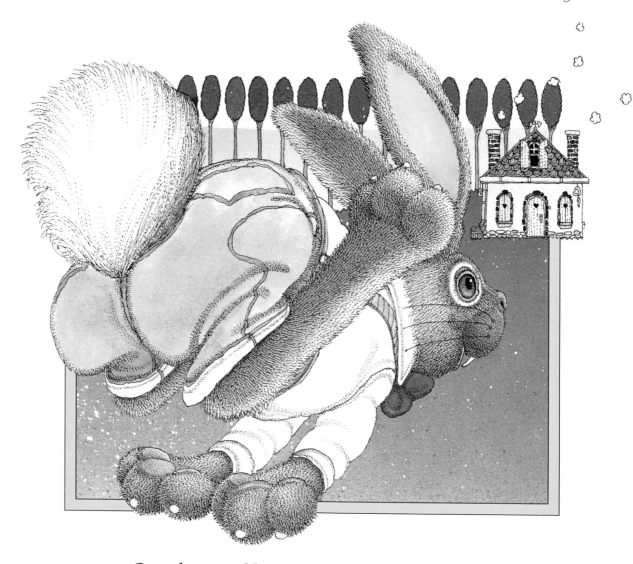

One day, a rabbit was hopping through the forest very quickly and hopped right up to the little house.

"Well, how do you like that! A little house! I wonder who lives here?"

This time, the butterfly answered for everyone.

"We live here. I am Bernice the butterfly. And living with me are Millie the mouse, Fred the frog, and Rudy the rooster. And who are you?"

"Me? I am a rabbit. My name is Richie. Please, let me in. Hurry! A fox is chasing me."

"Well then, come in, come in! We will find room for you."

17

And all five started to live together.
One day a big storm came. It was dark
everywhere. It thundered. The rain poured down in
buckets. And right in the middle of the terrible
storm they suddenly heard a growl at the door.

19

"Hey there! Who lives in this little house?"
Then there was such a hard knock on the door
that it almost cracked right down the middle.

20

But this time Bernice the butterfly was careful.
She opened the shutters only slightly, looked out
and fluttered.

"Millie the mouse, Fred the frog, Rudy the
rooster, Richie the rabbit, and I, Bernice the
butterfly, live here. Who are you?"

"I am a bear. My name is Bartholomew. I am wet right down to my skin and I am chilled to the bone. Please let me in so I can dry and warm myself."

22

"I would be happy to let you in," Bernice the butterfly said, "but you are a big bear and we do not have enough room for you. Sorry."

But Bartholomew the bear had nowhere to go! Where in the world could he dry himself? He climbed up to the roof to be near the warm chimney.

24

But the roof of the little house could not hold such a heavy load and it collapsed under him! Luckily, no one was hurt since everybody had time to run out of the house.

When the rain stopped and the sky turned blue, they all gathered around to look at what was left of the little house.

"Now we don't have our little house anymore and we have no place to live," Millie the mouse said, and she began to cry.

26

The bear was embarrassed. He came over to them and said:

"I am sorry! Will you please forgive me?"

"Of course we will forgive you," they all replied, "but where are we going to live now?"

"I know. I'll help you build a new house," Bartholomew replied.

"What a wonderful idea!" they exclaimed happily. "Let's build a bigger house so you can live here too."

So together, they started to build the new house. And Bartholomew worked the hardest of all. He worked from morning to night!

At last their beautiful new house was finished. It was known for miles around as the biggest little house in the forest. All six lived there happily— Bernice the butterfly, Millie the mouse, Fred the frog, Rudy the rooster, Richie the rabbit, and Bartholomew the bear. And they even had plenty of room for visitors.